KU-078-401

HERE
COMES
the
TRAIN

CHARLOTTE
VOAKE

WALKER BOOKS
AND SUBSIDIARIES

LONDON • BOSTON • SYDNEY

Every Saturday William, Chloe
and Dad go for a bike ride.
William sits on the back
of Dad's bike in his
little red seat.

They go across the golf course, through the woods, and out onto the footbridge.

The bridge is very high
and narrow, with railings
to stop people falling
over the edge.
And far below are
the railway tracks.
Dad lifts William out
of his seat and leans
his bike against the railings.
Sometimes Chloe has
a bit of trouble making
her bike stand up.

Then William and Chloe and Dad
look and listen for the trains.
It's very quiet and sometimes
they can see rabbits chasing
each other through
the bushes.

Sometimes workmen walk
along the railway with
shovels and spades
to mend the line.

Often other children and
people with dogs come
onto the bridge.

They all look at the signals.
When the lights change from
red to green ...

everyone on the bridge
hopes it means a train
is coming soon.

They all stare up
and down the line.

Then suddenly there it is,
a tiny speck in the distance!

William shouts,
"Here it comes...
HERE COMES
the TRAIN!"

Louder and louder,
nearer and nearer it comes!
Sparks shoot out
from its wheels!

All the children wave like mad.
The engine driver waves back;
he hoots his horn.
Beep-barp!

Beep-BARP

Everyone holds their
breath and ...

WHOOSH

under the bridge it goes!

Everyone's hair blows
in the wind.
The bridge rattles
and shakes.

Chloe SCREAMS because
she thinks it will fall down.
Everyone else screams
because they like screaming!

Afterwards,
when the train
has gone,
and it's quiet
again,

William,
Chloe and Dad
stand on the bridge
and wait ...

for the NEXT one!!!

Beep barp,

Beep - BARP

BEEP - BARP!

At night, when William
goes to bed, if he's very quiet,
he can still hear the trains
in the distance.
And he whispers to himself,
"Here comes the train!
Here comes the train!
Here comes the train!"

before he falls fast asleep.